THE PRINCE WHO WAS A FISH

THE PRINCE WHO WAS A FISH

by Jan Wahl

Illustrated by Robin Jacques

Simon and Schuster • New York

Text copyright © 1970 by Jan Wahl
Illustrations copyright © 1970 by Robin Jacques
Published by Simon and Schuster, Children's Book Division
Rockefeller Center, 630 Fifth Avenue, New York, New York 10020
First Printing
SBN 671-65122-6 Trade
SBN 671-65121-8 Library
Library of Congress Catalog Card Number: 76-124291
Manufactured in the United States of America

To
Doris
with
much
love

Once there lived a prince, Prince Proud Arm, who liked to go fishing. Not just on Saturday, for to a prince every day is Saturday, but every day in good weather. Soon the river in which he fished was being emptied of fishes at an alarming rate. The remaining inhabitants twisted their scaly tails in terror. Glittering objects would be dangled before their eyes, and one by one the fishes were hooked and yanked from the water like shooting stars.

At the bottom of the river lived a great silver-colored Flounder, a wise, clever fish. He wore a pair of magnifying spectacles in order to watch out for the Prince's baits. The Prince was fond of dangling feathers, baubles and

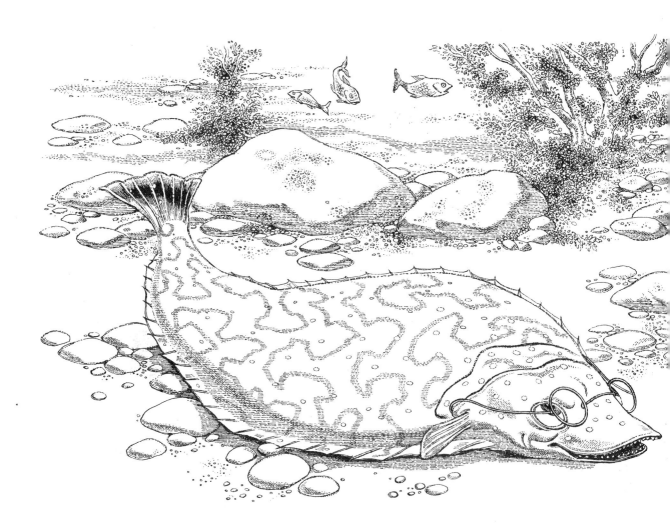

bright-flashing ornaments of every description and size. You never knew what he would use next with a hook or barb hidden inside.

But the Flounder peered with care through his spectacles and was clever enough to resist the tempting, pretty snares. Alone of the fishes he was not impressed by

bright-colored objects. He would pass by the Prince's bait, chuckle loudly, and swim off, triumphant and free. The Flounder was an enchanted fish, but not so enchanted that he didn't have to rely on his wits. (A Gypsy had given him this enchantment. She had stolen a valuable ring, and

might have been hanged if he had not swallowed the evidence.)

He was very clever and very wise, that Flounder! So, when many of the fishes had vanished, he still roamed in the water, magnificent, every scale gleaming.

11

Prince Proud Arm, young as he was, was famous for his strength and his love of sport. He was determined to land this slippery fellow. At night he tossed in his big bed as if it were a boat upon a storm-pitched sea.

Fishie, fishie, flat and wet!
I promise you—I'LL CATCH YOU YET!

he would shout aloud. Then he would fall off to sleep dreaming about the moment when he would haul in the great Flounder.

Each rainless and snowless morning the Prince would set forth in his richly painted boat, ready with his nets and his baskets of lures. Prince Proud Arm would drop an almost invisible line, woven from silk or the lightest, finest lion hair, spun so thin yet so strong it might have lassoed a herd of runaway buffalo. He would fasten to his line a bright feather or two, a fancy shell or a golden charm, and throw the line overboard, sitting with his head hanging over the water, watching for a glimpse of that clever, that famous, that uncatchable fish.

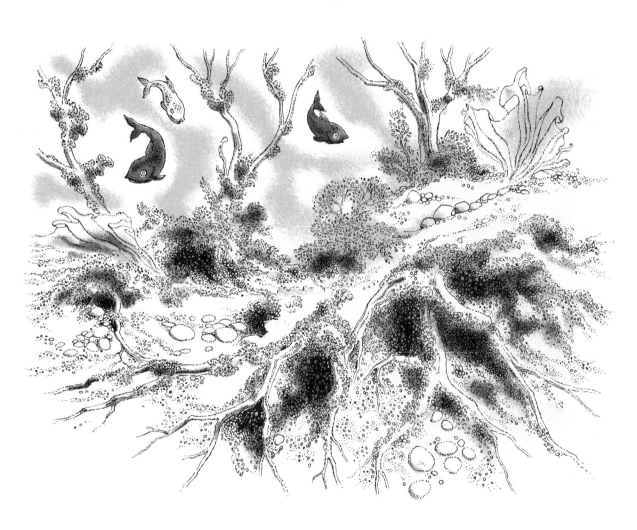

He would stare into the shadowy depths below,
watching the grasses that rolled along the bottom of the
river—the black, mysterious caves—the lichens that made
pictures upon the rocks.

From his drifting boat, water life seemed very

beautiful. To be able to swim all day long seemed an enviable treat. The Prince also wished he could fly like a hawk. But to be able to swim like a fish would be much better! He envied the Flounder his watery blue glorious world!

At the end of the line, one day, he fastened a gorgeous, glistening pearl with emerald wings fixed to it so that it looked like a giant dragonfly. Surely this would catch the Flounder!

But the Flounder as usual was not fooled and laughed

to himself. Bubbles of laughter rose up to the surface and
made a necklace around the boat. Then speedy loops and
curlicues that streaked across the river, wild and winding.
The Prince became so dizzy from it that he had to shut
his eyes. The Flounder laughed until his sides ached (and

since a flounder is *all* sides, he ached a lot).

By the time the Prince opened his eyes again, the fish had hidden himself in a safe deep grotto. The Prince packed up his gear and headed back to the palace. The fading orange-purple sun seemed to be winking at him.

Back in the palace, Proud Arm plunked himself down upon a velvet divan. He was so hot and angry he had to be cooled by ten servants with large palmetto fans.

Fishie, fishie, flat and wet!
I promise you—I'LL CATCH YOU YET!

20

he shouted, and he grew blue in the face, and kicked the
nearest servant.

The next day was bright and sunny. Daffodils fashioned
from delicate enamel and porcelain had been planted in
flocks along the river banks. Red rubies hung like cherries

in the royal orchards. No expense had been spared to show that this was a very rich kingdom.

The Flounder, below the water's surface, stretched his fins and yawned and prepared for another boring chase, which he would win, of course. He casually floated on his

left side and nibbled at a few choice grasses in a sunken
meadow. He skimmed over heaped-up rocks and laid some
watercress on the monument stone for his friend the
Trout, who had been caught by the Prince the week before.
The Trout had wanted to see a gleaming opal necklace up

close. The necklace had turned out to be a snare and the poor fish had been quickly hoisted out of his element. The Flounder could recall his friend flipping with his tail a last, sad Goodbye.

"That will never happen to me!" the Flounder declared. "I am too wise!"

Next he performed a loop-the-loop underwater with exquisite grace. He came up with a mouthful of sweet river moss, which he munched very elegantly. At that moment he glimpsed a mirror hanging nearby on a silver string.

The Flounder had never seen a mirror before. He looked at himself with admiration—at the impressive spectacles perched on his nose, at the glint of his shining scales, at the curve of his sleek, handsome tail. He sighed, pleased to recognize himself, and would have looked all day if at that instant a net had not swooped down and lifted him high into the air!

"Ha!" cried the Prince. "I've got you now, fishie!"

It seemed indeed he had. However, the Flounder was now able to use the small bit of enchantment given to him by the Gypsy.

"Proud Arm," the Flounder replied, "you have me, yet you have me not. This catch has its catch. I'm not ready for the frying pan!"

All at once, the grass on shore burst into song. It was only a trick, and it couldn't free the Flounder from the net. But it startled the Prince, who asked, "What do you mean?" The muscles in his arms ached while the Flounder danced about in the net.

At that moment a black, swirling cloud crossed over the sun. The water and the land turned chilly, and the sky above turned spooky gray with flashes of lightning, and the Prince was very much impressed.

"You and I," answered the Flounder, "are going to exchange places. You will henceforth lead the life of a fish underwater, while *I* will lead the life of a prince, on land. Now release me from this net and give me your cloak and crown."

"Suppose I don't want to do it?" suggested the Prince. The weight of the heavy Flounder in the net was beginning to make him pant and groan.

The Flounder concentrated with all his might, causing the grass to sing louder yet. It was enough to convince the Prince that he should not refuse, so he released the fish and gave him his cloak and crown. The Flounder donned the royal garments and regally steered the boat toward shore, leaving the Prince to sink into the water.

Down dropped Proud Arm, falling like a great weight

into inky depths. Blackness swelled around on every side until he settled like a stone at the river's bottom.

Then the sun above sprang out again, marvelously lighting up the water. A rainbow blazed forth in a shimmering arc. At first the water muffled up his eyes and ears and he had to squint to see anything. Then he learned to listen as fishes do, and his eyes became used to

looking in the water, and he found he could breathe
normally because of the enchantment.

Up ahead he soon heard the sounds of a terrible
battle. Fierce roars and sharp, dreadful screeches caused his
sensitive ears to ring and the water around to shake and jiggle.

A Dogfish and a Catfish were fighting, tossing each
other furiously end over end.

Pebbles flew. Marsh grasses in bunches were torn up by the roots. The two leaped and tumbled and wrestled and showed no sign of stopping their battle.

"Wait, hold on a minute!" the Prince called out. He tried to snatch the pair by their slippery tails. "What is happening here?"

Surprised by this question, the Dogfish and the Catfish stopped at once and turned to him.

"We are fighting," announced the Catfish, licking her fins. "Anybody can tell that!" She rolled her quick eyes dramatically, purring to herself. Then she hissed at him.

"Yes! Certainly we are fighting," repeated the Dogfish.

"How about getting out of our way?" Then he barked sharply and wagged his fins, and barked again.

"If it is true you are fighting," observed the Prince, "and it seems true enough, there must be a *reason* for it."

The Catfish carefully preened herself. "Look, we don't have to fight over ANYTHING. We fight every day at this

time, in this place!" The Dogfish nodded in agreement.

The Prince sat down on a sunken rock. He was still having to get used to wetness everywhere. "Then you fight because it pleases you. I understand that, for I do mostly what pleases me. However, couldn't you choose something else instead? Such as playing dominoes,

perhaps?" He himself was a champion player. When he wasn't fishing he would sit in the palace playing dominoes with the Chancellor of State.

"Dominoes?" the two inquired, wide-eyed. "What might they be?"

"Never mind," said Prince Proud Arm, who had no

special skill at explaining. Instead, he whistled to the Dogfish. "Dogfish, come along with me. If you are clever, I'll call you Fido."

Although it meant giving up his daily fight, the Dogfish accompanied the Prince, trotting in a fish trot behind the Prince's heels. They left the Catfish angrily meowing to

herself because she had no one to fight with. Each word turned into a bubble, and soon they could no longer see her for the mass of bubbles.

The Prince scratched his nose. Where to go?

"When in doubt underwater," he said, "I suppose it is

best to set a course straight ahead." So he did, with the Dogfish Fido tagging after him.

Fido showed him the secrets of the water kingdom. He showed off the collection of strange-shaped pebbles, guarded by three strong Pickerels, and where the fallen

rain was kept, and the famous fish schools. He showed him how the top of the sky looks from below even in daylight (very dark and star-filled), and they listened to the frogs lamenting, "CHEER UP! CHEER UP! CHEER UP!" Next, Prince Proud Arm was led to an immense

carved wood chest. Around it many small fishes danced
in a flurry.

"Fido," he asked the Dogfish, "what is that?"

"That?" answered Fido with pride. "The Flounder's
chest of treasures. Sacred objects he collected from above."

The Prince dashed forward, shooing off the hovering little fishes. Eagerly, the Prince lifted the hinged lid.

He expected to find souvenirs of his fishing lures. But to his astonishment he discovered that instead of topaz brooches, silver pieces, diamonds, and pink and yellow jade, the box contained the following:

Worn cooking pots with burned bottoms. Sadly
battered, leaky pans. Discarded twisted forks. Rusty spoons.
Broken dishes. Cracked, unusable bowls. All of which
had come from the royal kitchen, dumped by the royal
Footmen! As quickly as these objects had been thrown into
the river, they had been gathered and stored away by the

fish folk under the Flounder's direction as the greatest
treasures of all, since they did not spangle or sparkle and
seemed to have no use whatever.

Fido paddled back and forth, admiring this queer
display. The small fishes crowded around, thrilled.

Gingerly, slowly, Prince Proud Arm shut the lid. He

sat on a moss clump with his chin in his hands, mystified. Common things that tumbled into the water were hoarded as if flung down from Heaven. What was rare was rare.

Prince Proud Arm had always believed that a thing was worth exactly what you paid for it. He didn't want to disappoint Fido, so he pretended to be dazzled. "Beautiful!

Beautiful!" he cried almost convincingly, thinking that would please his little companion.

It did. Fido the Dogfish barked and wagged his fins. The Prince arose, and together they wandered on in the twisting river.

A bass family raced by and circled noisily around, showing off their stripes. They swam out of sight in a

parade. A group of eels wriggled by, twisting into amazing shapes, singly and together. On land the Prince was the show-off. Here he was not!

Great-Grandfather Tortoise ambled forward to inquire in which direction he was heading. "You are heading straight into the reeds," Fido replied to the Old One.

"Then that's fine," Great-Grandfather Tortoise drawled.

"Because I want to take a nap in a few days." And he creaked on, dragging his muddy feet.

Night fell swiftly. The water turned violet-blue and dark green. The creatures kept moving—moving ceaselessly. The Prince wished he were back in his warm, dry royal bed. He continued walking, seldom swimming, because it would

have made him more tired than he already was. He felt clumsy beside the eels, other fishes and turtles, which moved continually even at night.

In this place of clay, weeds and rocks, he knew he was the most awkward creature of all.

At length he sat on a stone seat until night had passed.

Morning shot down and was reflected through the water. Light blue, pink, light green. The Dogfish and the Prince soon came upon the Sturgeon, who was practicing his morning's flying. The Sturgeon liked particularly to leap high out of the water.

"Fishes and birds are alike," he suddenly announced. He swooped quickly, gracefully toward the travelers. "Sky and water are very much the same. They are simply large pieces of flowing space. Water's the heavier, and that is why it is on the bottom!" he said, executing a tailspin, some

flip-flops, and an upside-down Butter-On-Your-Back roll.

"Fishes and birds—that is, those who by nature soar and swim—are brothers, since they move the way they think," he continued. "When they are calm they glide. When they are frightened they flutter. If they are joyous they leap. If they are lazy they ride with the current. And so forth."

And with that bit of information, and no other, the Sturgeon bounded upward. In the twinkling of an eye he was out of sight.

"Strange fellow," declared the Prince, who was, at once, afraid to take another step. Should he glide? Leap? Or soar? He wasn't sure exactly which way he felt at all.

"Oh," explained Fido, "the Sturgeon often talks to himself like that. For lack of books to read, I guess. Nobody ever thinks to throw *them* in the river."

Still, what the Sturgeon had said was interesting, and the Prince mulled it over. *Were* birds and fishes freer beings than man? Immediately, the Prince and the Dogfish tumbled down a waterfall and were rushed, pell-mell, downstream.

"Catch your breath! Here we go! . . . Mother of Fish!"

cried out poor Fido, getting his tail fin wedged in a narrow space between two viselike rocks. "Don't worry, I'll join you presently! If I can! It's here today and gone today in the river," the Dogfish muttered wistfully.

Terrific veils of rushing water already separated

them. The Prince was about to try to swim back for his
friend. But up ahead he saw glittering in the water a great
enormous buckle encrusted with the brightest of emeralds—
so he grabbed it. Whereupon in an instant he was hoisted
up into the air with dizzying, sickening speed. He had just

begun to think of the water as home. Was this the end?

It was the Flounder, of course, who had made the catch.

The Flounder was sitting in the royal fishing boat, looking very impressive. He wore a new pair of spectacles. The Prince was damp and shivering and dripped water.

"Then you haven't learned anything much," sighed the
Flounder while the Prince dangled at the end of the line.
"Since here you are, caught like any fish! While I've been
busy industriously setting your kingdom to rights. It has
fallen to pieces during your fishing trips! Don't you know
anything about your kingdom at all, or what trouble it has

been in? You might as well try to catch me again," claimed the Flounder, taking off the royal cloak and crown, unhooking the Prince and handing him his clothing. "I would rather take my chances below in a world without palaces and princes and frying pans to cook fish in."

Prince Proud Arm huddled beneath his cloak, his teeth chattering. Sheepishly he put the crown back on his own head.

"No, fishie, I don't want you now," he replied, thinking hard on the subject. "I don't believe I will care to drop a hook in the water again. I understand how easy and terrible it is to get caught!"

The Flounder prepared to dive below, to return to his watery sphere. "By the way," the Prince added quickly, "I wish you would look after my friend Fido, the Dogfish. His tail may still be wedged between two rocks."

"I will," said the Flounder. Then he dived in, leaving

behind only some circles widening, rippling through the water.

The Prince headed home, and the moon came up in the shape of a silver fish swimming across the sky. Swimming free, free, free.

A crowd of Footmen, with lanterns, stood on the river bank awaiting Proud Arm's return. "Your Highness, we were worried!" they called to him as he landed. "You have been looking and acting peculiar!"

"Is that true?" he exclaimed, and he laughed all the way into the palace. He stayed up all night making signs to put up, which read:

FEED THE FISH. NO FISHING ALLOWED. FISH ARE FRIENDS. FISHY IS NOT A BAD WORD.

And he tried to be as good a prince as the Flounder was.